HiCCUP HARRY

by Chris Powling
and Scoular Anderson

DUTTON CHILDREN'S BOOKS

NEW YORK

Text copyright © 1988 by Chris Powling
Illustrations copyright © 1988 by Scoular Anderson

Library of Congress Cataloging-in-Publication Data

Powling, Chris.
    Hiccup Harry/by Chris Powling and Scoular Anderson.—1st
American ed.
        p. cm.
    "Originally published in Great Britain by A & C Black
(Publishers), Ltd."—T.p. verso.
    Summary: Harry disrupts the school when he tries
to get rid of a bad case of the hiccups.
    ISBN 0-525-44558-7
    [1. Hiccups—Fiction. 2. Schools—Fiction. 3. Humorous stories.]
I. Anderson, Scoular. II. Title.   89-23694
PZ7.P8843Hi   1990   CIP
[Fic]—dc20   AC

First published in the United States in 1990 by
Dutton Children's Books,
a division of Penguin Books USA Inc.

Originally published in Great Britain by
A & C Black (Publishers) Ltd.

First American Edition   Printed in the U.S.A.
10 9 8 7 6 5 4 3 2 1

Do you know what a hiccup is?

This is the story of the worst hiccups I've ever had. Every kid in my school had to stop work because of them.

It happened when I was {HIC!} years old. Six years old, I mean.

The hiccups began when we were sitting cross-legged on the carpet in the book corner.

Ms. Hobbs was taking attendance.

5

"He has the hiccups," said Sharon.

"I can hear that," said Ms. Hobbs. "Now settle down, please. It's not that funny. Remember what we said yesterday about helping Harry behave himself? Okay, Harry?"

Ms. Hobbs gave me one of her
I-mean-it looks. She thought I was
fooling around again.

"Pull yourself together, Harry,"
she snapped.

"I don't want to hear any more of
those hiccups. You can control them
if you want to."

I was afraid to ask her how.

So when it was our turn in the
playhouse, I asked Tracy instead.

"It's simple," she whispered.
"You can make hiccups go away
by singing a song, Harry.
My dad told me."

"A song?" I said. "What kind of  song?"

"It doesn't matter. Any song will do."

This sounded crazy to me, but I didn't have a better idea.

Keeping my voice as low as I could,
I started to sing.

This made Tracy giggle.

"Shhh!" I hissed.

"But you're so funny, Harry," she said.

Humpty Dumpty had a great HIC!

By now Bernard and Sharon were
giggling too.

If I was quick, though, I might get rid of
the hiccups before Ms. Hobbs
heard me.

Half the class had the giggles by
this time.

They were crowding around the
playhouse to hear my singing.

Or maybe they wanted to hear my
hiccups. Whichever it was, they were

Ms. Hobbs was too late.

With a

CRASH!

CLATTER

and the loudest

Bonkety Bonk!

you ever heard,

the playhouse collapsed on top of
Tracy and me.

Ms. Hobbs wasn't very pleased.

At last

she dug through the mess.

Then she fixed me with another one of those looks.

"I might have known you'd be at the bottom of this, Harry. What do you have to say for yourself?"

Guess what I said?

You're right.

Which is why I was sent to the
nurse's office.

A big glass of cold water?

Terrif . . .

. . .HIC!

But where was the big glass

HIC! to put the cold water in?

It took me a long time to find one.

There was a glass on top of Ms. Frisby's big cabinet where I couldn't **HIC!** reach it.

Yes, I know I should have waited for Ms. Frisby.

She's our school nurse and she's never out of her office for long.

I was in a  hurry, though.
So I opened the cabinet doors.
I stepped on the bottom shelf.

And I stepped on the second shelf.

And I stepped on the third shelf.

The hiccup seemed to tip the cabinet
forward as I fell backward.

Now I stretched out my hand.

But the glass began sliding toward me . . .

I hit the ground in a shower of books

and cans and boxes

and old notebooks

and clothes from the lost-and-found

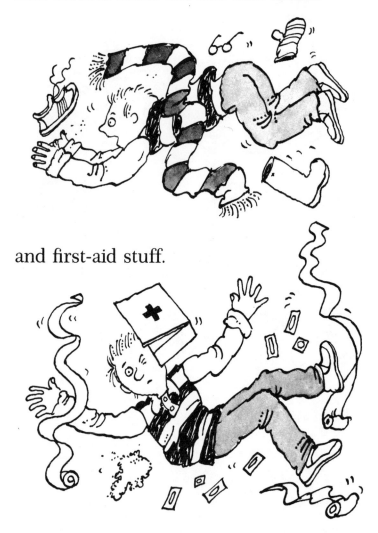

and first-aid stuff.

How the cabinet itself missed me I
don't know. It was the only thing
that did miss.

I felt like I'd been buried under a garage sale. And all because of my hiccup! It wasn't fair. Ms. Frisby was going to think I made the mess.

"Better get out of here, Harry," I told myself.

So I dashed into the hall.

I was halfway back to class when a big kid stopped me.

"What's the rush, kid?" he asked.

Usually I'd be too shy to talk to a
fourth grader, but he looked so friendly
I told him everything.

He especially liked the part about the
playhouse.

"That's great," he laughed. "You're
the funniest little kid I've ever met."

"But
I've
still
got
these

dumb
hiccups."

When the fourth grader had gone, I
looked down the hall. Where was there
room for a handstand? One side of
the wall was all windows.

The other side was covered with
paintings and drawings.

Except for one place.

There on the wall was an empty space next to a small glass box with a handle.

"That will do," I said. "I'd better make this my best HIC! handstand ever."

One

two

three

HIC!

45

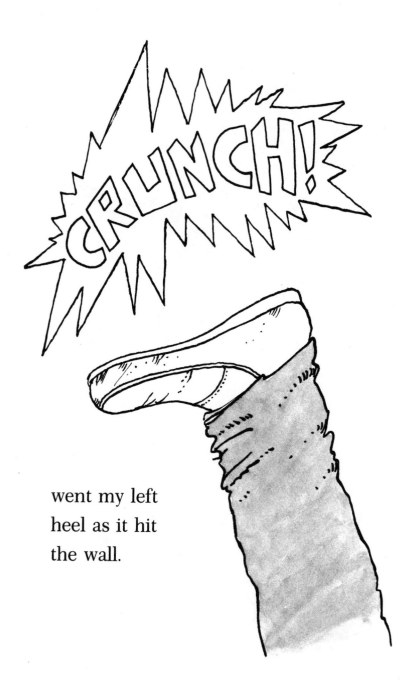

went my left
heel as it hit
the wall.

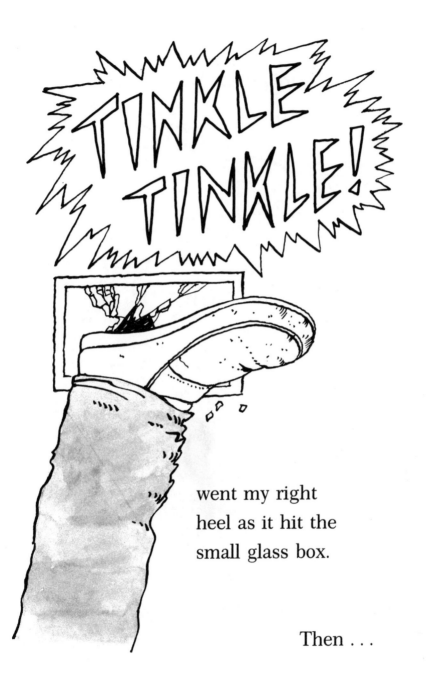

went my right
heel as it hit the
small glass box.

Then . . .

I heard doors opening, the shuffle of feet, and teachers getting kids into straight, quiet lines. It was a fire drill.

Everybody would have to stay out in the playground until our principal, Ms. Cadett, made sure the school was empty.

Somebody had set off the fire alarm, you see.

No, not somebody.

Suddenly I realized what had
happened. My hiccup had started
the fire alarm when my foot kicked the
handle on the small box!

I was
so scared
I froze
as stiff as
an icicle,
still upside down.

The school was silent now. Even the *dinga, dinga, dinga, dinga* had stopped.

I heard footsteps coming toward me. I didn't dare move. I knew right away who it was.

Harry?

It was Ms. Cadett.
I felt her eyes shift from me to the broken glass and back again.

When Ms. Cadett is happy she has a face like a smiley lion. Now, seen from the bottom end of a handstand, she looked to me like a growly lion.

"Wait for me in my office, Harry,"
she said. "I'd better get everyone
back into school again. They must
think the school is burning down."
In Ms. Cadett's office, I waited

and waited.

At last she came.

By now I was so terrified I kept my eyes on the carpet in front of her desk.

"Harry," she said. "I've been talking to Ms. Hobbs and Ms. Frisby. You've been causing quite a commotion this morning."

"It wasn't my fault," I wailed.
"Really, it wasn't. My hiccups
knocked over the playhouse.
And my hiccups tipped over Ms. Frisby's
cabinet. And it was my hiccups
that rang the fire alarm."

"Your hiccups did all that?" she asked.
"They must be pretty special hiccups.
May I hear one?"

"Okay," I said.

I stood there.

"Go ahead, Harry," said Ms. Cadett.

Still I stood there.

You can probably guess what my
problem was. My hiccups had
disappeared—yes, *disappeared*.

I couldn't believe it. Just when I
needed them, they were gone.

It was as if I'd never had a hiccup in
my life—as if I'd been pretending
about everything. What would
Ms. Cadett do to me now?

Suddenly . . .

Not me, no. The hiccup had come
from Ms. Cadett. When I looked up
I saw a huge grin on her face.

"That was a fake hiccup, Harry," she
said. "But I've had the real hiccups
all morning. Then the fire alarm
scared me so much they disappeared."

"That's when *my* hiccups went!" I said.

"Tell me about them." She grinned.
"And I'll tell you about mine."
Then she winked at me. I'd forgotten
that Ms. Cadett could be a
laughing lion.

Of course I had to help with
the cleanup—and promise
never to go near the fire alarm again.

The best part, though, was when
Mom picked me up from school.
Ms. Cadett got her to see
the funny side, too. We joked about
it all the way home.

Mom figures the next time I have the hiccups I'd better stay outside in our backyard. She doesn't want the house to fall down, she says.